Baby For The Tark Commander

Alien Baby Pact

Aurelia Skye and Juno Wells

Published by Amourisa Press, 2023.

JOIN JUNO WELLS' NEW RELEASE LIST!

Click on this link (or copy and paste it into your browser):

http://eepurl.com/bnMJL5

Join Kit's Mailing List[1] **(www.kittunstall.com/newsletter) to receive notification of new releases and access bonus chapters for your favorite books. You get free books just for signing up. If you prefer to receive notifications for just one, or a few, of Kit's pen names, you'll have the option to select which lists to subscribe to at signup.**

---

1. http://kittunstall.com/newsletter/

Blurb

RANA RELUCTANTLY ACCEPTS her duty as a proxy but is drawn to her mate. As their love develops, a growing rebellion threatens to tear them apart.

Like every other Earth woman in compliance, Rana registers for the proxy draft, praying she won't be matched with a Faction alien. Instead, she's quickly paired with Tark Commander Sarko D'sano. With handsome features and glossy white feathers, she's instantly drawn to him. He soon proves himself to be a gentle mate who wants a mate, not just offspring.

As she surrenders to the pull between them, planning to build a future with her alien mate, a rebellion stirs. Some are fed up with the draft and see it as slavery. They're getting more desperate and bolder, and they think they're rescuing women mated to the aliens. When they try to "save" Rana from Sarko, they have no idea what they've unleashed, or how far each of them will go to return to the other.

Seven years ago, the Faction agreed to save Earth from the vorathan invasion in exchange for Earth women giving them one year of proxy rights to act as a surrogate, since the aliens of the Faction faced a dwindling population. With the vorathans feared throughout the galaxy as bloodthirsty, vicious marauders, the Earth's government agreed.

That doesn't mean the women did.

Sometimes, you want to read about the entire alien empire and all its myriad twists and turns, immersing yourself in hundreds of pages of intrigue. And sometimes, you want to skip the frills and get to the main event. Juno and Aurelia are pleased to bring you a series of short, steamy romances about untouched human women making babies with their truly alien mates.

Chapter One

RANA TOOK A DEEP BREATH as she entered the Faction Embassy, her stomach fluttering with anxiety. Today was the day she'd been dreading—her twenty-first birthday, and the day she had to officially enter the surrogate registry. She'd put it off as long as she'd dared.

Like all women on Earth between eighteen and twenty-five, she was now eligible for selection by one of the aliens of the Faction. According to the agreement made seven years ago at the end of the Vorathan invasion, Earth owed a "debt" to the Faction, to be paid by providing human women as potential surrogates.

Rana thought it was an archaic custom, but she understood why the desperate leaders of her battered world had agreed to it. That didn't make walking through the doors of the Embassy any easier.

The sterile white walls and sleek metallic surfaces felt cold and imposing. She wished her best friend Priya could have come with her, but she had to do this on her own.

A severe-looking Faction official directed her to take a seat in the waiting area. Rana sat, perched nervously on the edge of the smooth silver chair. She watched as other young women entered, some scared like her, others nonchalant.

After twenty tense minutes, a proctor said, "Rana Shreveet?" Rana stood on trembling legs and followed the proctor down a wide hallway. She was directed to a small exam room containing complex medical equipment and told to sit on the table.

Moments later, a Mosaic doctor entered. Like others of his gene-spliced race, his appearance was an amalgamation of different alien species. He had dusky purple skin, a bald head, and large luminous orange eyes.

"Hello, Rana, I am Dr. Mikal." He introduced himself in perfect, lightly accented English. "Please relax. I know this process can cause anxiety, but it will be over quickly."

She tried to calm her breathing as he began the examination, which included a full body scan, retinal scan, and DNA sample. After confirming her good health, Dr. Mikal smiled kindly.

"There, all done. Your profile will now be entered into our database for potential matching. You are free to go and will be notified if you're selected."

Rana thanked the doctor and took the printed information packet he offered. She stepped outside into the sunny day moments later, finally able to breathe. One step down, though she had four more years of eligibility ahead of her.

Trying to push her worries aside, Rana strolled through the bustling market on her way home, picking up some greens to cook a special dinner. She wanted to make tonight nice for her parents. They had been devastated when receiving the letter reminding her she was almost out of time to register and still be in compliance with the law.

After dinner, she left her parents' POD to walk a few sites over to the POD she shared with Priya. Even seven years later, housing was scarce with so much of their city still in ruins from the Vorathan attacks.

She changed into her nightclothes and tried to lose herself in a historical K-drama on her datapad, but her mind kept drifting. What if she was selected? Would it be one of the giant Grimlocks or the frightening, cold-blooded Serps? It could be a Tark or an Alphan. Rana shuddered at the thoughts.

A soft ping drew her attention—an incoming video call from Priya, who was working the night shift as a nurse at the hospital. She accepted eagerly, ready to vent to her closest friend. Priya's face filled the screen, her large dark eyes full of sympathy.

"How did it go?" asked Priya, who had gone through her own registration almost five years ago. Her BFF was almost free and would be released from the proxy program on her next birthday.

Rana grimaced. "About as dehumanizing as expected. They scanned every inch of my body like a farm animal."

Priya shook her head, her thick braid slipping over one shoulder. "Ugh, I'm sorry. It was the same for me, but at least it's over now, right?"

"For today, but I'll have to live with this threat hanging over my head for the next four years until I'm twenty-five." Rana sighed, hugging her knees. "I can't have a boyfriend or any kind of normal life until then."

"I know. It sucks." She gave an encouraging smile. "At least the chances are still pretty low you'll actually get picked. I mean, there are billions of us and only a few hundred thousand of them. Try not to stress too much."

Rana nodded, wishing she shared her optimistic friend's attitude. "I hope you're right. I'll feel a lot better after your birthday passes next month with no match."

They chatted for a while longer until her eyes grew heavy, and her friend's dinner hour ended. After wishing Priya a good night, she curled up under a blanket, her mind churning with restless thoughts. Somehow, she had to find the strength to get through this.

TWO WEEKS LATER, RANA walked down the street with Priya, enjoying their day off together. They passed a sprawling refugee camp of PODs, tents, and makeshift dwellings. It was one of many that still housed those displaced by the invasion. The scars left behind would take lifetimes to heal.

Priya linked her arm through Rana's. "Let's not waste our free time. I'm taking you shopping."

She rolled her eyes dramatically. "Ugh, do we have to?"

"Yes. When's the last time you bought something new? We just got paid."

"Oh, all right." Unable to say no to her exuberant friend, she let herself be dragged toward the shops. She had to admit, it was nice to peruse and daydream a little, even if she couldn't justify buying much. After mostly browsing, they stopped to get dinner from a street vendor.

"It's so ridiculous," she said over noodles and what she hoped was pork. "My body doesn't belong to them just because of some archaic deal."

Priya nodded in sympathy. "I know, but maybe we'll both get lucky and never get picked."

"Hopefully," said Rana half-heartedly. She didn't share her friend's optimism.

OVER THE NEXT FEW DAYS, Rana tried to distract herself and not think about the possibility of selection. She threw herself into her work at the hospital, where she was an aide, and spent time with Priya. She also made an effort to visit her parents more often. As they shared meals together, her mother would sometimes tear up quietly and squeeze Rana's hand under the table. Her father attempted light jokes, but they came out strained.

During a visit, Rana found her mother crying softly in the kitchen. When Rana hugged her, all her mother said was, "I wish I could protect you." Though unspoken, Rana could feel their sorrow, knowing her future was no longer hers alone.

ONLY A WEEK LATER, a message flashed on her datapad—an official notice from the Faction Embassy. Rana's stomach dropped as she read the words: Selected for surrogacy service. Please report to the Embassy immediately for matching and assignment.

With trembling hands, she grabbed her coat and hurried out the door. This was really happening. In a matter of hours, she would meet the alien to whom she'd been matched. Her life would never be the same.

Nearly an hour later, she stood numbly in the waiting room, the words of the notice echoing in her mind. She'd stopped by to tell her parents, and they'd hugged her but had been unable to find any words of comfort. Priya had tried to reassure her as they vid'd goodbye.

"Maybe you'll get one a nice one, like a Brundle or a Tark," Priya had said gently.

Rana clung to her friend's words like a lifeline now. She watched as other stunned young women were ushered back one by one to meet their assigned Faction matches. The room was silent with everyone lost in their own worries and fears.

Finally, Rana's name was called. She stood on shaky legs and followed the proctor into a small conference room. A Tark sat at the table, finally revealing the species with which she'd been matched. He had skin so deep purple it was nearly black, large white wings folded behind his back, and white hair that flowed past his shoulders. His cat-like yellow eyes met hers, and he gave a small smile that seemed meant to reassure.

"Hello, Rana. I'm Commander Sarko D'sano. Please take a seat."

Rana sat carefully across from him, nerves and curiosity warring within her. Of all the aliens, she knew the least about the Tarks. He had a kind, almost artistic look to his angular features, and there was a birdlike quality in his features and sharp nose. He watched her closely, as if trying to gauge her reaction to him.

"I understand this is frightening, so I want to explain what will happen now. First, you'll receive a mild genetic modification to allow you to safely carry a hybrid pregnancy. Then we'll be bound for a one-year contract. I hope in that time we can get to know one another, and you will come to see this as an opportunity, not a burden."

She swallowed hard, trying to keep an open mind. She had no choice but to trust in fate now. Meeting his golden gaze, she nodded slowly. "I'm ready."

A proctor took her back to the medical wing for the genetic modification procedure. She laid tensely on the exam table as Quillin, the golden Mosaic Med Chief, explained how it would allow her to conceive and carry a viable pregnancy with Sarko's alien DNA. Though non-invasive, the idea of being altered on a genetic level made her deeply uneasy, but she stayed silent since there was no alternative.

Afterward, a different proctor led her to Sarko in a small ceremonial chamber. As promised, they went through the ritual binding. Their wrists were loosely tied together with a silken cord as they signed the year-long contract on a datascreen. Rana's hand trembled as she added her signature.

"The contract is complete. You may leave the Embassy," said the officiant.

Sarko gave her a sympathetic look. "I'm on leave, so I thought we could spend these next several days getting acquainted before leaving for my rotation on Baxa."

"Your homeworld?"

"The Faction's new homeworld. Like everyone else, the Vorathans destroyed mine." His yellow gaze turned amber for a moment in his grief. Then he held out a hand. "We can go to my ship, or we can go to your dwelling."

"I live in a POD with my friend, Priya."

He nodded. "I suggest we use my ship. I have it docked until my leave ends, and it's easily accessible."

"Okay."

As they turned to leave the ceremony chamber, a news report flashed on a nearby vidscreen, showing protesters clashing with Embassy security. "The rebellion grows stronger every day," said Sarko with a frown, "But I'll keep you safe."

She nodded silently. She knew little of the rebellion against the Faction surrogacy pact, but their actions would probably just make things worse. She steeled herself and followed Sarko out of the Embassy and into the unknown future ahead.

RANA STEPPED ONTO THE bridge of Sarko's sleek starship, her eyes widening at the viewport showing the city skyline. "It's bigger than I expected."

He came up behind her. "Yes. The ship is basically self-contained. I know it doesn't seem like much parked among the other ships here at the Embassy docking station, but when you see the stars..." His sharp face formed a wide smile that was oddly appealing.

"Is it true you can fly through space without a suit?" she asked, recalling a fact from the Embassy packet.

"Yes. We evolved in the vacuum of space, and our bodies adapted to survive in it. We're the only ones of the Faction who have that ability, and your genetic modification to bear my offspring won't confer that."

"That's a relief," she joked weakly.

Sarko chuckled. "You should rest. I know you must be exhausted after everything that's happened. The ship will be parked here until we leave for Baxa in ten days."

Rana shook her head. "I'm actually hungry. Do you have a synthicator?"

"Of course." He led her through the narrow hallway and into a bigger room. "This is the galley, and the synthicator works like the one in your POD, though in Tarkisian rather than English."

Rana studied the glowing symbols on the screen. "What does this one mean?"

"*Duschtak* and *hornid*—a frog and beetle-type dish is the closest translation."

Rana wrinkled her nose. "Not exactly what I had in mind."

"Try this one."

She tapped the symbol he'd indicated, and a plate of fragrant curry and rice appeared. "Thank you."

He gestured for her to sit at the small table as he synthicated his own meal. She eyed it with a hint of wariness when he sat the gelatinous green blob on the table. Seeing her look, he said, "It's a traditional Tark dish called *mehyk* and similar to your sushi."

She took a bite of the spicy chicken curry, watching as he ate his meal with apparent enjoyment. "How long have you been part of the Faction?"

"Since I was a child. My people were among the first to join after our planet was destroyed. It was either that or die out."

"Your parents survived the Vorathan invasion of your homeworld?"

His expression flickered with grief. "Only my mother. She died a few years ago."

"Oh, I'm so sorry."

He looked brooding for a moment before he returned to eating. "I've learned to accept it."

Rana finished her food, feeling more relaxed. "Where will I sleep?"

Sarko showed her the sleeping quarters, which contained a bed and storage compartments. "I'll sleep on the bridge. If you need anything, I'll be there."

Rana nodded, suddenly overwhelmed with exhaustion. "I think I'll try to sleep."

"Good night, Rana."

A short time later, she laid down. The bed was surprisingly comfortable and far better than the thin cot in her POD. She let her mind wander as she listened to the soft hum of the engine while she drifted into sleep.

Chapter Two

HAVING HER ABOARD WAS like a low-grade itch he couldn't scratch. His senses had tuned to her, and her pheromones wafted toward him. He could join her in the sleeping quarters right then and insist on breeding her, but he wanted to win her over. He hoped to end up with more than a child from their arrangement. He wanted a mate, and so far, Rana suited him well, though he didn't know enough about her yet.

That would come in time, but she already smelled divine, making his cock harden and causing him to shift in the captain's chair. It wasn't designed for sleeping, especially with him being almost seven-feet tall and having a twelve-foot wingspan when he unfurled them.

He decided to meditate instead of going to the sleeping quarters. He needed to clear his mind and focus on the task at hand. Attracting Rana. The mating urge was strong, but he'd be damned if he'd give in to it. He wanted her to choose him as a mate, not just be his surrogate.

He closed his eyes and focused on his breathing, letting the tension ease from his muscles. As he slipped into a meditative state, his mind calmed, and his thoughts stilled. Time seemed to slow, and peace washed over him.

When he opened his eyes, he felt refreshed and ready to face the day. He heard her stirring and decided to join her.

"Good morning," he said, entering the sleeping quarters.

"Morning," she said with a yawn.

"Did you sleep well?"

"Surprisingly, yes. I thought I'd be tossing and turning all night."

"I'm glad to hear it."

She stretched, and he admired her curvy form. She was beautiful, with her dark hair tumbling to her shoulders and her brown eyes sparkling with intelligence.

"I guess we have a lot to talk about," she said, breaking the silence.

"Yes. Let's go to the galley and have breakfast. Then we can discuss our plans."

They sat at the table and synthicated their meals. Rana chose scrambled eggs and toast, while he opted for a bowl of porridge.

"So, how does this work?" she asked, taking a bite of her eggs.

"We'll be spending the next few days getting to know each other and preparing for our journey to Baxa. Once we arrive, we'll settle into our new home and begin the process of conceiving a child."

"And what happens after that? Will I stay on Baxa with you?"

"That's up to you. You're welcome to return to Earth if you prefer, but I would like you to consider staying with me when your year ends, or after you have our baby."

"Why?" she asked, looking puzzled.

"Because I think we could be good together. We don't have to be just surrogates. We can be mates." He saw her alarm and instant rejection of the thought.

"I can't imagine being happy away from my family and Earth, Sarko." She looked regretful as she told him that.

He tried not to show his discouragement. "Perhaps you'll be surprised. Tell me what you would do on a typical day?"

"I worked as an aide at the hospital until receiving my proxy notice, so I resigned." She tipped her head slightly. "I could introduce you to my parents."

He nodded. "You are lucky enough to have both still living?"

She nodded. "Yes, though my brother, Aarav, was killed in the Vorathan attack."

His hearts beat in sympathy. "I lost two nest-mates in the invasion along with my father." He sighed. "My mother survived a few years but never lived to see the Faction push back the Vorathans."

Her lips pressed in a thin line. "I'm sorry."

"It was a terrible time. The Vorathans came with no warning, destroying entire cities and killing millions of my people. It was only through the intervention of the Faction that we were able to save those who remained."

"I know the stories. The Vorathans attacked without provocation, slaughtering billions of innocents. The Faction arrived in time to stop the genocide and drove the Vorathans into exile."

"Yes, and did the same for Earth."

She looked troubled. "At the cost of forcing all young women to be surrogates."

"Potentially only." He shook his head. "It isn't ideal, but our species are all so decimated, and you have far more females than we do."

"I know, it's just...not something I ever imagined doing."

"No, but it's an obligation that comes with living in this society. You can't always have your way."

"I suppose not." She looked at him. "Do you enjoy being a soldier in the Faction?"

He shrugged. "Most of the time. It's not an easy life, but it's important work. I'm proud to serve."

"You must see a lot of different worlds and cultures."

"Yes, and it's fascinating. There's so much to learn and experience in the universe." He smiled. "That is one aspect I very much enjoy about my service, but I admit I'm longing to settle into my homestead and put down roots for a while."

"I wonder if I'll ever get to travel like that."

He smiled. "For safety, we'll have to pass several jump points to reach Baxa, so we can explore some of those planets along the way. Once I've claimed a homestead and began the process of making it habitable, I can take you on short trips to some of the planets near Baxa."

She smiled. "I'd like that."

They spent the rest of the day talking and learning more about each other, and he found himself nervous as the time to meet her parents for dinner approached. When she changed from jeans and a T-shirt to a *sari*, he was surprised at what a difference it made in her appearance. "You are beautiful in anything, but I like the touch of formality this gives you."

She flushed, which was visible despite the copper hue of her skin, ducking so her shoulder-length hair obscured her face. "Thank you." As she passed near him, her skin brushed his.

His eyes widened, and he chirped softly as his cock surged. Her eyes widened, but not with fear. She seemed...curious, and perhaps aroused?

"We should go. My parents will be expecting us."

"Yes." He forced himself to calm down and follow her out of the ship.

She led him through the streets of the city, pointing out landmarks and explaining the history of the area. He listened attentively, enjoying learning more about her world.

As they entered the POD, he could tell it was a tight squeeze for the three of them in the tiny common room.

"Mom, Dad, this is Sarko. Sarko, my parents, Roshan and Anitra."

"Welcome to our home," said Roshan with a polite nod.

"Thank you. It's a pleasure to meet you."

Anitra smiled, though there was a hint of sadness in her eyes. "Please, sit. Dinner is almost ready."

Sarko took a seat at the small table, trying not to bump into anything. He was aware of Rana's close proximity as she sat beside him. The scent of her was intoxicating, and he had to resist the urge to lean closer.

Roshan brought over a pot of steaming curry and set it on the table. "Here we are. Eat up."

Sarko helped himself to the fragrant dish, savoring the spicy flavor. "This is delicious. Thank you."

Anitra smiled. "It's an old family recipe, though the synthicator does the cooking these days."

They ate in silence for a few minutes before Roshan spoke again. "Sarko, tell us about yourself." His eyes were dark and probing. "What do you want from my daughter?"

"First and foremost, a family." He made no effort to hide his desire to have a child and carry on his line. "I also want to be a good partner to Rana, to provide for her and support her in whatever she wants to do."

Roshan nodded, seeming satisfied with his answer. "And what about your people? What do they think of this arrangement?"

"My people believe that all life is sacred, and that all beings should be treated with respect and compassion. We don't believe in slavery or coercion, and we value free will above all else. Rearing a nestling is the highest achievement of my people. Our children are our everything." He cast a quick glance at Rana. "Though we are still utterly devoted mates, and that's a bond that lasts for life."

"I'm sure Rana will appreciate that," said Anitra, giving her a warm smile. "Isn't that right, Rana?"

Rana nodded, her cheeks flushing. "Yes, I think it's very admirable."

After dinner, they sat in the living room, continuing to talk and get to know each other. Sarko could tell that Rana's parents were still worried about her, but he hoped they would come to see he was genuine in his intentions.

"You have a lovely home," he said, glancing around the small space. "I can see why Rana enjoys living here."

Roshan smiled, pride evident in his voice. "Thank you. It's not much, but it's ours."

Anitra nodded. "It's a good place to raise a family."

"I live with my friend Priya a few PODs over these days," said Rana a moment later.

He nodded at the information but continued to look at her parents for a long moment. "I hope to make a good home for Rana on Baxa."

"I'm sure you will," said Anitra. "I must confess to fearing our daughter's fate when we first heard she'd been matched."

"I was scared too," said Rana softly.

"And now?" asked Sarko, almost holding his breath.

She smiled. "Now, I'm hopeful." She reached out and touched his arm. "I feel like I can trust you, and that means a lot to me."

He covered her hand with his, feeling the warmth of her skin against his scales. "I will do everything in my power to deserve that trust."

After a little more conversation, it was time for them to leave. Rana hugged her parents, and Sarko thanked them for their hospitality. As they walked back to the ship, Rana slipped her hand into his, and he felt a surge of happiness.

"Thank you for coming with me," she said softly.

"I'm glad I could be there. Your parents seem like good people."

"They are." She paused. "I know they're still concerned about me, but I think they can see that you care about me."

"I do," he said, stopping to face her. "I know this is only the beginning, but I want you to know that I will try to make you happy. I want this to be a partnership, not just an arrangement."

She smiled up at him, her eyes shining with emotion. "I want that too."

As they boarded the ship, he was hopeful about the future. Perhaps this could be the start of something wonderful for both of them.

HE MADE HIMSELF AS comfortable as he could in the captain's chair again that night, torturing himself with images of Rana stripping the *sari* from her body to reveal tantalizing curves and copper-brown skin. She wasn't a lot like him physiologically, but either the injection had modified her to pique his sexual interest as much as his affection, or she was just naturally enticing.

He suspected it was the latter. Her scent had been driving him mad since the moment he'd met her. It was sweet and spicy, with a hint of musk that made him think of the wild forests of his homeworld. And the way she moved, graceful and elegant, like a dancer.

He groaned softly as his cock hardened, straining against the fabric of his pants. He couldn't take it anymore. He had to have her. He got up from the chair and made his way to the sleeping quarters, pausing outside the door. He heard her breathing, steady and even. She was asleep.

He hesitated, not wanting to wake her. With a soft sigh of disappointment, he turned to go back to the bridge.

Then he heard her stir. "Sarko?"

He turned back to face her, his heart racing. "Yes?"

"Come here."

He obeyed, moving to stand at the foot of the bed. She was sitting up now, her hair mussed from sleep.

"What is it?" he asked, his voice husky with desire.

She bit her lip, her eyes meeting his. "I can't stop thinking about you."

He moved closer, his body responding to her words. "I can't stop thinking about you either."

She reached out and took his hand, pulling him down onto the bed beside her. He went willingly, his pulse racing.

"We could get to know each other better, but..."

"But what?" he prompted.

"I feel like I already know what I need to, at least enough to begin the mating part of our bargain." She gave him a tentative smile. "I'm comfortable knowing you'll be an excellent father if I happen to conceive."

He lifted her hand. "Do you want me though? Not just to fulfill your contract?" His breath caught in his throat as he awaited her answer.

She nodded, her eyes dark with desire. "Yes."

Chapter Three

SHE LEANED FORWARD tentatively, feeling shy and nervous. She was inexperienced and had never even really experienced passion before, let alone for a Tark, but Sarko was handsome and kind, and she could trust him.

He met her halfway, pressing his lips against hers in a gentle kiss. His lips were soft and warm, and she felt the heat of his body as he pulled her closer. She melted into his embrace, her hands exploring the hard planes of his chest and shoulders. He was muscular and strong, and she sensed the power in his arms as they wrapped around her. His wings fluttered but didn't expand.

Their kisses grew more passionate, and she moaned softly as his tongue slid between her parted lips. She tasted the sweetness of his mouth, and she wanted more.

She ran her hands through his thick white hair, tugging gently as she deepened the kiss. He growled low in his throat, a sound of pure male satisfaction.

He broke the kiss, his golden eyes burning with desire. "You're so beautiful. I want you so badly."

"I want you too," she whispered, her voice trembling with anticipation.

He kissed her again, his hands roaming over her body, caressing her breasts and hips. She gasped as he cupped her ass, squeezing gently.

"You're so soft," he said, his voice rough with need.

"So are you." She ran her fingers over the smooth scales covering his skin. He purred when she stroked along the outer feathers on his wings. "But hard too." She giggled slightly as she daringly brushed her hand against his huge bulge. Her eyes widened. "How different are you from a human man...down there?"

"Let me show you." His voice was a low growl as he pushed her back onto the bed.

He stood and removed his clothing, revealing his naked body to her. She stared at him, transfixed by the sight of his powerful muscles and the large, ridged cock that jutted proudly from his hips. Strange bumps protruded from the area up and down the bottom of his shaft. "Why...?" She gestured to the line of ridged bumps.

"Seed sacks. It's where I keep my semen, and when I come, it flows into you from several sources." The explanation was matter-of-fact, but his eyes gleamed with hunger.

She swallowed, her mouth suddenly dry. "I see." She wondered how many times she'd have to orgasm to ensure conception. She had a feeling she'd find out soon.

He climbed onto the bed, kneeling between her legs. He gazed down at her, his eyes filled with desire as he leaned down to kiss her again. His tongue passionately dueled with hers as he spent a moment ripping off her tank top and underwear.

His tongue was long, flexible, and muscled. She closed her eyes and caressed it with her own. He tasted like spice and cinnamon, and she couldn't get enough.

She arched her back, pressing her bare breasts against his chest. He growled, a sound of pure masculine pleasure, and she shivered with excitement.

His hand trailed down her stomach, and he cupped her mound, stroking her wet folds. She gasped, her hips bucking as he found her clit and rubbed it.

"You're so wet, but you must be absolutely drenched to be able to accept my cock." He started stroking her clit as he spoke. A moment later, his tongue glided from her lips to her neck, and he gently nipped her as the very tip of his talon dragged ever so gently across her clit.

She cried out, her body shuddering as waves of pleasure washed over her. She writhed beneath him, her hips grinding against his hand. He kept stroking, gradually increasing the pressure as he slipped his thumb into her slick channel. She appreciated how flexible his hand was with his differently configured joints as he stroked her clit, gently fingered her pussy, and moved his head down, arching his back and spreading his wings as his tongue swirled around one of her nipples.

"Sarko," she cried out, head thrown back as she rode the waves of ecstasy. Her inner walls clenched around his thumb, and he growled with approval.

"That's it. Come for me," he rasped, his voice thick with passion. "I want to feel you come on my hand."

She climaxed, her body shaking with the force of her release. Her juices flowed freely, coating his hand as she cried his name.

He withdrew his thumb and licked it clean, his eyes never leaving hers. "Mmm, you taste delicious. I can't wait to taste more of you."

He lowered his head and readjusted his body so his tongue could reach her slit. It darted out to lick her swollen clit. She gasped, her hips jerking as he began to suck on it. He was relentless, sucking and licking her sensitive bud until she was writhing and moaning with pleasure. She clutched at his head, her fingers tangling in his hair as she rubbed her pussy against his face.

He chuckled, the vibrations sending shivers of delight through her body. "You're so responsive, my mate. I love it."

He continued to feast on her, his tongue sliding in and out of her dripping core. She whimpered, her thighs quivering as she teetered on the edge of another orgasm. "Sarko, please. I need you inside me. I need your cock."

He raised his head, his eyes blazing with yearning. "Not yet. I want to taste your pleasure again."

He returned to his task, his tongue lapping at her clit. She sobbed with frustration, her body aching for release. He continued to drive her higher and higher, until she was a quivering mass of need. Finally, he gave her what she craved.

With a final, hard suck on her clit, he sent her over the edge. She moaned, her body convulsing as she came. He lapped up her juices, growling with satisfaction.

"Give me all of your pleasure. I want to drink every drop."

She collapsed, spent and sated. He rose to his knees, his cock protruding proudly. It was massive, with a bulbous head. He had no testicles, which surprised her, but he didn't need them with his seed sacks.

"Are you ready for me, my mate?" he asked, his voice thick with desire.

She nodded, her eyes fixed on his impressive member. "I'm a little scared. Will it hurt?"

He looked pained. "For a few minutes, no doubt."

He crawled up her body, his weight pressing her into the mattress. She felt the heat of his skin, and the hardness of his muscles as he positioned himself at her entrance.

"Relax, my mate," he whispered. "I'll be gentle." He eased the head of his cock into her tight channel.

She gasped, her eyes widening at the stretch. It was painful, but there was a strange pleasure too. He pushed deeper, and she moaned, her body adjusting to his size.

"There." He grunted, his voice strained. "I'm all the way in."

"Oh, god." Her inner walls clamped around his massive girth. "You're so big."

He growled a sound of satisfaction. "And you're so tight. You feel amazing."

He began to move, slowly at first, then picking up speed as he found his rhythm. She clung to him, her nails digging into his back and feathers as he thrust into her. The pain quickly faded, replaced by an intense pleasure that built with each stroke.

"Sarko." He moaned, her body arching as he drove into her.

He growled, his pace increasing. "Take my cock. Take all of me."

The room was filled with the sounds of their bodies joining, their cries of pleasure echoing off the walls. She felt herself approaching the edge again, and she urged him on. "Yes, Sarko. Yes. Don't stop. Please don't stop."

He gripped her hips, his talons digging into her flesh as he pounded into her. She cried out, her body tensing as she came.

He roared, his cock pulsing as he released his seed a moment later. Multiple jets of hot fluid filled her, and she shuddered with pleasure.

He held tightly to her, looking deeply satisfied. "With all I've given you, surely you will conceive, Rana."

"I hope so." She wanted to give him a child.

He smiled, his eyes gleaming with affection. "I want to see you round with my child. You're everything I could ever dream of in a mate. I am honored to be yours."

She blushed, her heart swelling with joy. "I'm honored to be yours."

They stayed tucked together, basking in the afterglow of their lovemaking. He held her close, his body warm and comforting. She felt safe and loved in his embrace, and her heart overflowed with happiness.

She drifted off to sleep, content in his arms. Tomorrow, she would be able to truthfully tell Priya the sex was amazing, and she had far fewer reservations about spending a year with him. She already suspected their joining would be for far more than a year.

Chapter Four

THREE DAYS LATER, SHE said, "I need you to meet Priya. She's a much tougher judge than my parents." She gave him a small smile.

He looked intrigued. "I must earn her blessing?"

"I hope you will and can, anyway. She's like an older sister to me."

"I'd be honored to meet your friend."

"Good." She smiled. "Today is her day off, so I'll send her a vid message to see if she wants to meet somewhere. Our POD is tiny, and you'd swallow all the available space." She evaluated him, unable to hide her hunger as she had the thought.

He chuckled. "If you keep looking at me like that, we'll accomplish nothing but more mating."

She grinned. "I can't help it. I'm addicted to you."

He smiled, looking pleased with himself. "I'm glad to hear it. You're irresistible to me as well."

She flushed, her cheeks heating. "I'll send the message."

"I'll try not to distract you."

She laughed, knowing it was futile. He was a constant distraction, and she loved it. While he went to change, she vid'd Priya, whose worried face filled the small screen.

"Are you still alive?" asked Priya, mostly humorously.

"Yes, and I have news. I'd like you to meet Sarko. He's...amazing."

Priya's eyes narrowed. "Amazing? What's he done to you?"

She laughed. "Nothing bad. I promise. Just meet us at the cafe in an hour. Trust me."

"Okay, but if you don't show, I'm going to hunt you down and drag you out of that ship."

"I'll be there. I swear."

"All right. See you in an hour."

Rana ended the call and turned to find Sarko standing behind her. "Is she suspicious?"

"Very. She's convinced you've brainwashed me or something, I guess." She tilted her head. "Isn't that one of the rebellion's claims?"

He shrugged. "I don't pay attention to them. About your friend... How do we convince her otherwise?"

"I think we have to show her. She's not easily swayed, but she just wants me to be happy."

"I see." He nodded. "I will do my best to win her over."

"I know you will." She smiled up at him, her heart full of admiration and affection. "Now, let's go meet my friend."

They left the ship and made their way to the coffee bar, arriving a few minutes early. A large crowd had gathered around the block and intersection, and it left her uneasy. "Once we find Priya, we should go somewhere else."

He looked surprised. "Why?"

She gestured to the group, and they all wore some kind of face-coverings. It wasn't unusual to protect oneself from pollution with a mask, but something about them left her unsettled.

"I'm not sure. I just have a bad feeling."

"We can leave if you wish."

"No, we can't. Priya will think you're kidnapping me if we do."

He frowned. "I suppose that's true."

They waited for a few minutes, but there was no sign of Priya. Rana's unease grew, and she glanced nervously at the crowd.

"Maybe she's late."

"She's never late." Rana's voice was tight with worry. "Something's wrong."

Suddenly, the crowd surged forward, surrounding them. They were yelling and waving signs, their faces contorted with anger.

"Rana," shouted Priya, waving her arm as she forced her way through the crowd. "Get out of here."

"What's happening?" Rana asked, confused and frightened.

"It's the rebels," said Priya, grabbing Rana's arm. "They're protesting the Faction."

Rana's eyes widened. "But why?"

"They don't want humans to be taken as proxies anymore. They think it's slavery."

Rana shook her head. "It's not slavery. It's an agreement between our governments." Though she'd had similar thoughts before meeting Sarko.

"It doesn't matter. The rebels don't care." Priya tugged on Rana's arm, trying to pull her away. "We have to go."

She resisted, looking back at Sarko. He was surrounded by the protesters, their angry voices rising in a crescendo of rage.

"Move," Priya insisted, tugging harder.

She resisted. "Not without my mate."

A hard hand grabbed her other arm, and she turned her head. It couldn't be Priya.

"This one is that thing's mate," said the man holding her arm.

She knew it was a man by his bulk and deep voice, though he'd obscured his face.

"She's probably been brainwashed," said a smaller, slighter figure, also with her face covered. "Let's liberate her."

"No." Rana tried to break free, but the man held her fast, pulling her from Priya's grasp.

"Don't struggle," said the small woman. "We're trying to save you."

Rana strained harder, but the man's grip was like iron. He dragged her away from Sarko, who was being attacked by the mob.

"Sarko," she cried out, reaching for him.

He lunged for her, but the protesters blocked his path. He fought against them, but there were too many.

She watched in horror as the rebels overwhelmed him, dragging him to the ground. She screamed his name, but her voice was lost in the chaos. She saw a glimpse of Priya trying to get to her before the crowd blocked her view of her best friend as well.

The man holding her arm pulled her away, and she stumbled after him, her eyes still fixed on Sarko. She continued to resist until something jabbed her in the neck. It was sharp and painful. A hypodermic.

Her vision blurred, and her limbs felt heavy. She slumped against the man, who smelled like sweat and grease, her mind reeling. The last thing she saw before darkness claimed her was Sarko lying motionless on the ground, blood streaming from his wounds.

SHE WOKE IN A DARK room with a throbbing headache and blinked, trying to clear her vision. She was lying on a cot in what appeared to be a makeshift infirmary. There were other people in the room, but they were all strangers.

She sat up, groaning as the movement made her head spin. She put a hand to her temple, feeling a lump and a tender spot.

"You're awake," said a familiar voice.

Rana turned to see a blonde woman standing near her. Her voice was recognizable as the one who'd told the man to take her. "I want out of here."

She frowned. "I'm Natalia, and I want to help you. We have our own formula to counter the genetic modifications, and it will clear up your confusion."

Rana reared back, holding her stomach. "You can't. I might be pregnant, and that would kill my child."

The woman blinked, looking impassive. "You can't really want to be a broodmare."

"I want to be with my mate."

"He's a monster."

Rana bristled. "He's not. He's kind and gentle."

Natalia's expression softened. "You're still under the influence of whatever they did to you. You'll see the truth in time."

"I won't. I love Sarko, and we're having a baby." Rana was adamant, and she hoped the rebel wouldn't harm her unborn child, if she already carried one.

"You're delusional," said Natalia, "But we'll keep you safe until you come to your senses."

She glared at her. "I'm not staying here. I'm going to find Sarko."

"We're helping you."

"No, you're making a decision for me, just like the government has. You're not any better than the politicians who signed the agreement if you don't respect my choice." She stared intently at the woman's sea-green eyes.

She expected stubborn defiance or pity. Instead, slow comprehension appeared in Natalia's expression. "You really do love him, don't you?"

She hesitated only a second before nodding. She shouldn't have known him long enough, but her heart was already sure. "I do. Please let me go before someone else tries to 'save' me."

"I can't," said Natalia softly.

"You seem to be in charge," said Rana with an air of challenge.

Natalia bit her lip and looked around. "I can't believe I'm doing this," she muttered as she gestured for Rana to follow her.

They were in an underground tunnel system of some sort. "What is this place?"

"Old subway system," said Natalia. "We use it to move around undetected."

"Why do you need to do that?"

"Because the government is corrupt, and they want to control everyone."

"Maybe, but maybe they didn't see much choice either. And not all the aliens are like the Vorathans. The Tark and others aren't. They want peace."

"Maybe, but they still demanded our women in payment for their protection. That's slavery."

Rana hesitated. "It could be, but I think they make it as consensual as they can. It's complicated."

She didn't sound convinced. "I guess."

They walked in silence for a few minutes before she spoke again. "Can I contact Sarko somehow, so he knows I'm safe?"

"Once you get out of the tunnels, your vidscreen should work, if you have one."

"Thank you."

"Don't thank me yet. I could get in a lot of trouble for this."

"I appreciate it. I really do." She took a deep breath. "It's for the best anyway, because he'll find me. If I'm already gone, your people might be safe from his wrath."

Natalia turned down another tunnel, flipping on a light on her utility belt. "That's not exactly reassuring..." She trailed off, scowling. "What's that noise?"

"I don't hear anything." Even as she said it, Rana felt a low vibration overhead.

"Shit. It's a Faction ship. More than one maybe." She turned to Rana. "Run straight ahead until the next tunnel. Turn right and then left, and you'll see the light to guide you outside." Without another word, she turned and ran past Rana, obviously planning to warn her friends.

Rana took off running, following the directions Natalia had given her. She reached the end of the tunnel and turned right, her heart pounding. She turned left and saw the faint glow of daylight up ahead. She sprinted toward it, her breath coming in ragged gasps.

As she reached the exit, she heard an explosion behind her. The tunnel shook, and dust rained down from the ceiling. She didn't stop to look back, instead pushing herself to run faster. She burst out of the tunnel and into the sunlight, blinking against the sudden brightness. She still had her vidscreen, and as soon as she cleared the tunnels, she used it to raise Sarko.

His face filled the screen, and he looked like vengeance personified. "Are you injured?"

She shook her head. "Call off the bombing or whatever."

"I cannot. You're mine, and they took you. They must pay the price for their transgressions."

"I'm fine. No one hurt me, and I'm waiting for you to come get me." She zoomed out some to show him she was uninjured. "See? No harm done. Just a little nap and a chat."

He scowled. "The Faction enforcers are already here. Arrests are inevitable, but I'll try to ensure they don't use unnecessary force." The screen went dark.

She stood there for ten minutes, confused about what was happening. She heard a ruckus inside the tunnels but wasn't about to go back in there. Suddenly, Sarko's ship appeared before her, barely fitting on the street as he set it down and came charging out the ramp.

She ran to him. He scooped her up in his arms and carried her into the ship, his wings flapping with urgency. He set her down in the command center and began checking her over.

"Did they hurt you? I'll destroy them all if they did."

"No, they didn't. I'm okay. Really. I was more worried about you."

"Me?" He seemed genuinely surprised.

"Yes. The crowd was attacking you, and I was afraid you were badly hurt."

He smiled. "I'm tough, my mate. It takes more than a handful of misguided humans to injure me."

She hugged him tightly, relief washing over her. "I'm so glad you're okay."

He kissed her forehead gently. "You're safe now. I'll never let anyone take you again."

She smiled up at him. "I know. I trust you. You're my mate, and I love you."

His eyes widened, and he pulled back to stare at her. "You...love me?"

She nodded. "I do. I love you, Sarko."

He embraced her fiercely, his wings wrapping around her. "I love you, too. You're my mate, and I'll always protect you."

She rested her head against his chest, enjoying the feel of his arms around her. She was safe and loved, and that was all that mattered.

"What will happen to Natalia and the others?"

He shrugged. "I don't know. Until taking you, they've kept their demonstrations mostly peaceful. They've crossed a line. I assume one of the first things they'll do is check to see if any of the rebels are proxies who've shirked their duty."

"Will the rebels be punished?"

"Probably. The government will probably consider them traitors. It's likely the rebels will be treated as such."

She sighed. "I hate that so many lives will be ruined because of me."

He stroked her hair. "It's not your fault. The rebels made their choice. It's unfortunate you were caught in the middle, but it's not your responsibility."

She nodded. "I know, but I can't help feeling guilty. So many people have been affected by this."

He smiled. "And I've been affected by you. You've brought joy to my life, and I'll be forever grateful."

She smiled. "You've changed my life too. I'm so glad I met you."

He kissed her gently. "Let's say goodbye to your people and leave early for Baxa. I want you safely to myself as soon as possible."

She smiled. "I'd like that, but what about my family?"

"You can vid them, or we can visit in person. I'd like to be off this planet soon though."

"I'll visit them today, and we can leave tomorrow."

He seemed mollified. "That is acceptable as long as you promise tonight is mine."

She smiled. "Tonight, and every night after."

31

Chapter Five

TO AVOID ANY POSSIBLE danger of lone Vorathan ships hovering in chartered space, they had to take a series of jump points over the period of a few days to reach Baxa. Sarko spent the entire journey with his mate, and he was in awe of her. She was intelligent, funny, and passionate, and he couldn't get enough of her. Their passion for each other burned hotter and brighter with each passing day, and he was certain he'd found his perfect match.

At the midpoint of their jumps, he rerouted them. "I promised to show you some wonders along the way to Baxa," he said with a smile as he punched in the coordinates for a planet that was mainly beach and surf. "I thought you'd enjoy the chance to relax."

"I'd love that." She smiled at him. "I can't wait to see it."

He grinned, his heart swelling with joy. "Then we'll go." He pushed the button to activate the jump, and the stars stretched into streaks of light around them.

A short time later, they landed on a lush, tropical island, and he watched in amusement as Rana ran down to the water's edge, squealing with delight when the waves crashed against her feet.

"Come on," she called, beckoning to him. "The water's perfect."

He joined her, wading into the cool, clear water. He wrapped his arms around her waist and lifted her off her feet, spinning her around as she laughed.

"This is amazing," she said, gazing out at the ocean. "It's so beautiful here."

"It is," he agreed, setting her on her feet and kissing her deeply. "Almost as beautiful as you."

She blushed, smiling at him. "You're pretty handsome yourself, you know."

He chuckled. "I'm glad you think so."

"I do." She kissed him again, her hands roaming over his bare chest. "In fact, I think we should take advantage of this private beach and get naked."

He grinned. "I like the way you think, my mate."

They stripped off their clothes and swam in the water, laughing and splashing each other. He chased her through the waves, catching her and pulling her into his arms. They made love on the shore, their bodies entwined in the sand.

Afterward, they laid on a blanket, watching the sunset. She snuggled against him, her head resting on his shoulder. "I could stay here forever," she murmured.

He stroked her hair. "We can if you wish. This planet is unclaimed."

"That would mean giving up your homestead on the Faction homeworld." She sat up, tracing her fingers down his muscled abdomen before gently stroking his feathers. "I'd never ask you to do that."

"You're not asking. I'm offering. The Faction will understand, and I'm not due for another Earth rotation for four years."

"I don't want you to give up anything for me."

"I'm not. I'm gaining everything." He rolled onto his side, propping himself up on his elbow. He gazed down at her, trying to project all his devotion. "I am gaining you, my mate."

She smiled, her eyes shining with happiness. "I'm gaining you, my mate."

He leaned down and kissed her, his lips brushing hers in a tender caress. "I'll always be yours, Rana. I love you."

She returned his kiss, her arms wrapping around his neck. "I love you too, and staying here is just a fantasy. I want to see your homeworld."

"We can return here anytime you wish," he said, his voice husky with emotion. "I want to share everything with you."

She smiled, her eyes full of love and trust. "I feel exactly the same."

They spent the rest of their time on the beach exploring each other's bodies and making love in the sun and the surf. When it was time to leave, he felt a pang of sadness, but they would return to this paradise again someday.

As they flew away from the island, he vowed to bring her back as often as she wished. She was his mate, and he would give her anything she desired.

WITH A FEW OTHER DETOURS, it took almost two weeks to reach Baxa. They reported in to claim their homestead tract, and he flew them the allotted hectares. A POD waited for them. "It's not much," he said almost apologetically as they disembarked.

She smiled. "It's wonderful and will be amazing with some hard work." She gave him a teasing glance. "I think we'll need an extension though if that POD is only for two people."

"Yes, it is." His eyes narrowed. "Why? Do you wish to have your parents come to stay with us? I'd be happy to try to arrange that."

Her eyes sparkled with excitement. "That wasn't what I meant, but that would be amazing."

"I'll see what I can do." He pulled her into his arms, kissing her deeply. "What did you mean?"

"I'm pregnant, Sarko."

He froze, staring at her in shock. "You are?"

She nodded, a smile spreading across her face. "Yes. We're going to have a baby."

He swept her into his arms, twirling her around. "I'm overjoyed, my mate. You have made me the happiest male alive."

She laughed, clinging to him. "I'm so glad, because I'm thrilled too."

He set her on her feet and kissed her again, his heart bursting with joy. He was going to be a father, and he couldn't wait to start their life together on Baxa.

Epilogue

TRUE TO HIS WORD, SARKO had traded in a few favors and somehow pulled enough strings to allow her parents a refugee pass to Baxa. They soon had a POD on the same land, and she was glad to have her parents nearby, especially with her pregnancy.

It was happening faster than a typical human pregnancy, and she was a little nervous. She couldn't hide that as she tried to explain it to her mother. "From what I understand, the baby will be born in a sack-like membrane, almost like an eggshell. It'll crack with some effort, and then he or she will emerge."

Anitra looked stunned and slightly horrified. "Then do you sit on it like you would a chicken egg?"

Rana laughed. "No. The incubating stage happens in my body." She rubbed her large stomach, which was pointier and more oval-shaped than it would be with a human baby. "The Faction resources and the Mosaic doctor at the Hub say it's no more painful than giving birth to a human baby."

"How long now?" asked her father, looking nervous.

"Any time." She looked around. "Which is why I hope Sarko returns soon." He'd made a last-minute trip to the hub, citing a need for some kind of urgent supplies.

Her mother and father traded a look.

"What?" she asked with suspicion.

"Nothing. Will the baby nurse like a human child?"

"Yes. The development is roughly the same timeline, but you should expect your grandchild to have wings and clawed feet." She smiled.

Anitra looked unbothered. "I'm simply grateful to have a grandchild."

She rubbed her stomach. "I feel the same way..." She trailed off as Sarko's ship returned.

When the ramp lowered, she stared in shock as Priya sauntered down it and rushed toward her. "What are you doing here?"

"Your mate arranged it as a surprise." Priya grinned. "I'm allowed to stay until the birth and for a month afterward."

Rana turned to see Sarko striding toward her. "Is this true?"

"It is. I know how much you miss your friend, and I wanted to make you happy."

She threw her arms around him. "You've made me happier than I ever dreamed possible."

He smiled, his eyes full of love and affection. "I'm glad, my mate."

They shared a tender kiss, but she abruptly pulled back at a lurching sensation in her abdomen. "Oh."

He frowned. "Oh?"

"I think it's time." She looked at Priya. "You couldn't have come at a better hour."

"Perfect timing." Priya smiled.

Sarko picked Rana up and carried her to the POD. "Should I send for a Med assistant?"

She shook her head. "We have them available if we need them, but it's supposed to be easy enough."

It took a few hours of labor and intense contractions, allowing Rana to learn it wasn't easy by any means, but as the egg sack finally slid out a few hours later into Sarko's waiting hands, it was worth every moment of discomfort, since the pain blockers couldn't entirely eliminate all discomfort.

He held the egg reverently, and she saw their baby moving inside it. "Do we crack it now?"

"We do, but carefully." Sarko used the tip of a talon to puncture the shell, and a tiny foot kicked through the hole. He broke the rest of the way through, and Rana reached out to catch the infant as it tumbled out.

Their daughter was perfect, with Sarko's golden eyes and Rana's dark hair. She was also covered in a fine layer of downy white feathers.

"She's beautiful," Rana whispered, tears of joy streaming down her face.

Sarko leaned over and kissed her. "She is, just like her mother."

"I…" She trailed off with a moan. "Oh, I don't think it's over."

He gripped her hand. "You have another egg?"

She nodded, knowing it was always possible. Sometimes, Tark females birthed clutches of up to five, but the most a human woman had carried was three. She hoped they could stop with two.

Moments later, the second egg slid out, and he handed her their daughter so he could crack open the egg to free their son.

"See if there are anymore," she said, only half-joking.

He looked and lifted his head. "I don't see anything else."

She let out a huge sigh of relief and then swapped babies so she could examine her son. He was identical to his sister, and both were healthy and perfect.

"What will we name them?" she asked, looking up at Sarko.

"I was thinking we could name our daughter after my mother and our son after your brother."

"I think that's a lovely idea," she said, her heart swelling with love.

"Our daughter is Yarinka, and our son is Aarav."

She smiled, cradling the twins close to her breast. "I love those names."

"I love you, my mate," he said, his voice thick with emotion.

"I love you too," she said, her eyes filling with tears of happiness.

They kissed, sealing their bond with a promise of love and devotion for the rest of their lives.

"I can't believe you did all this for me," she said, her voice breaking with emotion.

"I would do anything for you," he said, his voice filled with conviction. "You're my world, and I'll spend the rest of my life showing you just how much I love you."

She smiled, heart overflowing with joy and love for her mate. "I guess we should let in the others to meet the new arrivals. My parents are impatient, and Priya came a long way for this."

He nodded but kissed her. "They can wait a few more minutes."

She smiled, leaning in for another kiss. "I agree."

They lost themselves in each other's embrace as they celebrated the birth of their children. It was a moment of pure joy, and Rana was filled with appreciation for her mate and the life they were building together.

About Juno

JUNO WELLS GREW UP on Florida's Space Coast, watching the shuttles take off from Cape Canaveral. When she hit college, her childhood fantasies about space travel turned highly romantic. Now her mind reels with space adventures of fantastic alien lords in distant galaxies, and the earth women they love.

Wells' stories explore the complex, sensual relationships between inhabitants of different star systems. There are always happy endings just as there is always a new world to explore.

Have a comment? Make first contact with Juno at authorjunowells@gmail.com.

About Aurelia

AURELIA SKYE IS THE pen name *USA Today* Bestselling author Kit Tunstall uses when writing science fiction romance, paranormal romance, and paranormal women's fiction. It's simply a way to separate the myriad types of stories she writes so readers know what to expect with each "author."

[Website](1)

---

1. http://www.kittunstall.com

Did you love *Baby For The Tark Commander*? Then you should read *Baby For The Grimlock General* by Aurelia Skye and Juno Wells!

She's been drafted to be a surrogate for the alien.

Violet Jones discovers she's been matched to a Grimlock general. She'll accompany the huge alien general to his home world. She only has to give him a year to woo her and act as his surrogate before she can walk away. At first, she's sure she can't give the massive alien what he wants, but he's completely contrary to what she expects. He's tender, caring, and obsessed with ensuring her pleasure and ability to accommodate him. Soon enough, the idea of leaving him seems crazier than the possibility of staying.

Seven years ago, the Faction agreed to save Earth from the Vorathan invasion in exchange for Earth women giving them one year of proxy rights to act as a surrogate, since the aliens of the Faction faced a dwindling population. With the Vorathans feared

throughout the galaxy as bloodthirsty, vicious marauders, the Earth's government agreed.

That doesn't mean the women did.

Sometimes, you want to read about the entire alien empire and all its myriad twists and turns, immersing yourself in hundreds of pages of intrigue. And sometimes, you want to skip the frills and get to the main event. Juno and Aurelia are pleased to bring you a series of short, steamy romances about untouched human women making babies with their truly alien mates.

Also by Aurelia Skye

Alien Baby Pact
Baby For The Brundle Commander
Baby For The Serp General
Alien Baby Pact Compilation
Baby For The Grimlock General
Baby For The Palantir Chief
Baby For The Alphan Captain
Baby For The Mosaic Med Chief
Baby For The Tark Commander

Alien Baby Pakt
Alien Baby Pakt Zusammenstellung

Celestial Mates
Wrong Place, Right Mate
Destined For The Drakari Warlords

Cybernetic Hearts

Mated To The Cyborg General
Claimed By The Cyborg Commander
Fated For The Cyborg Officer
Meant For The Cyborg Captain
Baby For The Cyborg General
Cybernetic Hearts: Complete Series

Dazon Agenda
Written In The Stars
Alien's Babies
Diplomatic Affairs
Moon Madness
Across The Stars
Emperor's Assassin Bride
Dazon Agenda: Complete Collection

Future Fairytales
Hooked

Guerriers Blessés
Chassé
Inlassable
Marqué
Justice
Compilation Guerriers Blessés

Marids und Gedächtnisverlust
Teufelsgeschäfte Und Schwindelzauber
Happy Ends Und Neuanfängen
Höllenhunde & Mistelzweige

Hell Virus
Catching Hell
Surviving Hell
Bleeding Hell
Raising Hell
Sharing Hell

Howls Romance
The Jaguar Alpha's Forbidden Lover
CEO Wolf Shifter's Surprise Twins

Northstar Shifters
Northstar Heir's Scarred Mate

Olympus Station
Station Commander's Surrogate
Alien Prince's Secret Baby
Security Agent's Alien Bartender
Olympus Station Compilation

SpicyShorts
Music In My Heart
Kilted Tentacle Monster: A Search for True Love

Sweet Escapes
Hook & Wendy

The Haunting of Clara Gray
Ghostly Awakening

Three Crones Inn
Vastly Inn-proved
Ghastly Intentions
Grave Inn-tervention
Ghostly Inn-heritance
Three Crones Inn Compilation

True North
True North #1: Death & Deception
True North #2: Rescued & Revelations
True North #3: Fire & Ice
True North #4: Enemies & Lovers
True North #5: Truth & Tiranog
True North #6: Fight & Flight

True North #7: Love & Loss

Wounded Warriors
Relentless
Marked
Justice
Wounded Warriors Collection
Hunted

Standalone
Reluctant Companion
Princess By Mistake
Fire Lord's Assistant
True North
Dragon Laird's Witch
Alien General's Rebel Consort
Tempted By Demons
Enemy Combatant
Grotesquerie
Mistaken Bounty
Wahre Richtung
Power Surges & Amorous Urges
Taken By The Orc General
Compilation Alien Baby Pact

Also by Juno Wells

Alien Baby Pact
Baby For The Brundle Commander
Baby For The Serp General
Alien Baby Pact Compilation
Baby For The Grimlock General
Baby For The Palantir Chief
Baby For The Alphan Captain
Baby For The Mosaic Med Chief
Baby For The Tark Commander

Alien Baby Pakt
Alien Baby Pakt Zusammenstellung

Dazon Agenda
Written In The Stars
Alien's Babies
Diplomatic Affairs
Moon Madness
Across The Stars
Emperor's Assassin Bride

Dazon Agenda: Complete Collection

Galactic Alphas
Alpha's Omega
Buying His Omega
Claiming His Omega
Galactic Alphas Compilation

Standalone
Alien General's Rebel Consort
Compilation Alien Baby Pact